Hippity Hop's
MATH PUZZLES

I know where the answers are! Page 32!

A Grosset & Dunlap ALL ABOARD BOOK®

Spilled Beans!

Help Hippity Hop find his jelly beans before Spot does! Can you find
2 purple jelly beans,
3 pink ones,
4 yellow ones,
5 red ones,
and 6 green ones?

"Uh-oh! Here comes Spot!"

Copyright © 1996 by Margaret A. Hartelius. All rights reserved. Published by Grosset & Dunlap, Inc., a member of The Putnam & Grosset Group, New York. ALL ABOARD BOOKS is a trademark of Grosset & Dunlap, Inc. Registered in the U.S. Patent and Trademark Office. THE LITTLE ENGINE THAT COULD and engine design are trademarks of Platt & Munk, Publishers, which is a division of Grosset & Dunlap, Inc. GROSSET & DUNLAP is a trademark of Grosset & Dunlap, Inc. Published simultaneously in Canada. Printed in the U.S.A. Library of Congress Catalog Card Number: 96-76449
ISBN 0-448-41302-7
A B C D E F G H I J

Hippity Hop's
MATH PUZZLES

By Margaret A. Hartelius

Grosset & Dunlap, Publishers

Lunch Time

Hippity Hop forgot to put his name on his lunch bag.
Which one is his?

Hippity Hop's lunch bag has:
5 jelly beans
1 lettuce sandwich
2 carrots
1 pretzel

①

②

③

④

Draw a circle around
Hippity Hop's lunch bag.

Clothesline

Show Hippity Hop what comes next.
Draw a circle around it.

①

②

③

Here Spot!

Hippity Hop has called his dog for dinner.
Look who showed up!

Help Hippity Hop find the real Spot.
Spot has 5 spots.

Big Time

Hippity Hop wants to buy the biggest fruits and vegetables.

Draw an X on the biggest one in each box.

Rabbit Reunion!

Hippity Hop's family is having a reunion.

I didn't know we had so many relatives!

How many rabbits are at the party?

Lots of Blocks

Hippity Hop used lots of blocks of different shapes to make this building.

How many △ blocks do you see? ☐

How many ⌒ blocks do you see? ☐

How many ☐ blocks do you see? ☐

Write the number in each box.

Look-Alikes

Hippity Hop needs you to help with these designs.

Make this   look like this

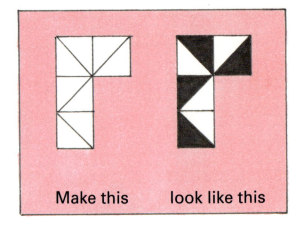

Make this   look like this

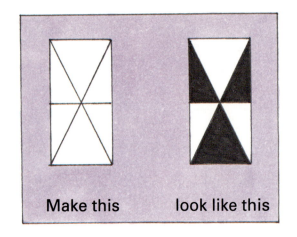

Make this   look like this

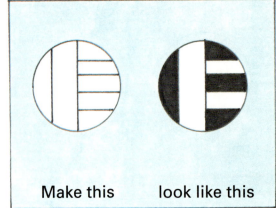

Make this   look like this

Spaceship Spaces

Use only 4 colors to color this spaceship. Next-door spaces must be in different colors.

Like this

Hippity Hop's Home Video 1

Birthday Balloon

Draw an arrow to where each picture belongs.

It's Raining! It's Pouring!

Hippity Hop needs his raincoat and rain hat, his boots and his umbrella. But he can't find them.

Can you help Hippity Hop?

Munch Time!

Uh-oh! Someone wants to join Hippity Hop for lunch!

To find out who it is . . .
Color all the spaces marked with 1 blue.
Color all the spaces marked with 2 green.
Color all the spaces marked with 3 brown.

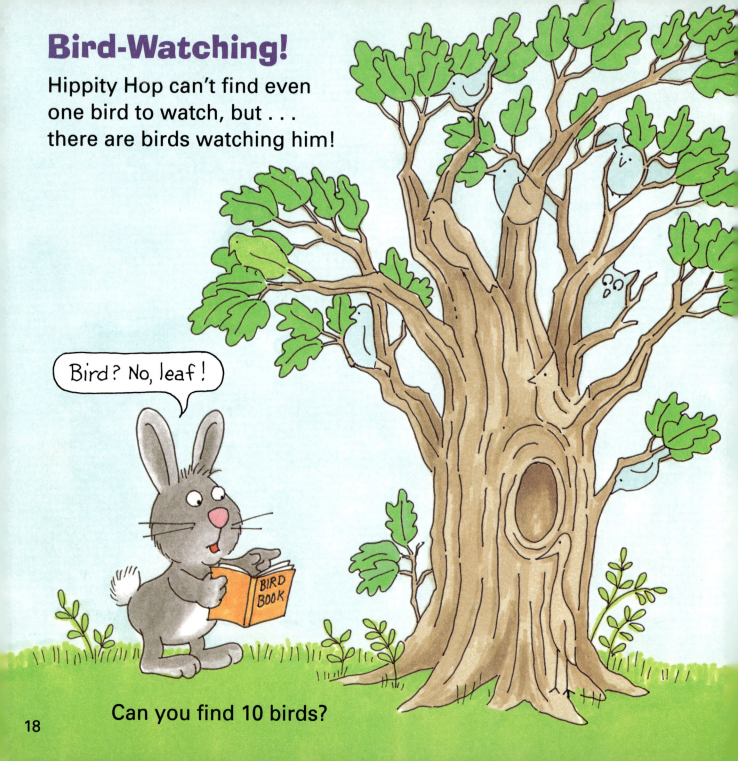

New Camera

Hippity Hop took photos of all these things.

① ② ③ ④

And this is how the photos came out.

Can you draw a line
from each thing to its photo?

What's Missing?

Help Hippity Hop find out what's missing in each set of pictures.

① ②

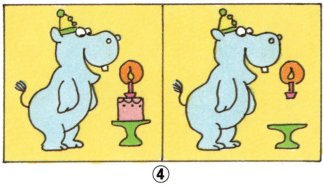

③ ④

Draw in the missing part.

Foursomes

Look at the 4 pictures in each square.
One is different. Make it the same.

Frog Race!

Follow each frog to see which one wins the race. Do not jump over any squares.

"I think the green one will win!"

"I can only go on the No. 1 squares."

"It's 2's for me!"

"Only 3's for me!"

1		2		3

1	1	5	2	2	3	3
1	4	3	9	2	5	3
1	1	1	2	2	3	3
1	6	1	2	2	3	4
1	1	1	3	3	3	3
5	2	4	3	6	7	1

FINISH LINE   FINISH LINE

Yipes! Stripes!

Hippity Hop is having trouble figuring out who is on his team.

Help Hippity Hop find the 6 players on his team. Draw a circle around each one on this page.

Catch it! Catch it!

Can Hippity Hop get to the ball?
Follow his path and find out.

Do <u>not</u> cross any green spaces.

Snow Fun

No two snowflakes are exactly alike . . . except in this puzzle! Help Hippity Hop find the twin snowflakes.

Draw a circle around them.

Silly Snowmen!

Hippity Hop made all of these snowmen, but only one is right.

Draw a circle around it.

Hippity Hop's Home Video 2

Snow Saucer

Draw an arrow to where these missing pictures belong.

Jelly Bean Machines

Hippity Hop loves jelly beans.
He wants to get the most jelly beans
for his money.

He only has 2 cents.
Which machine should Hippity Hop choose?
(Draw the number of beans
that will come out of each machine
when he puts in his 2 cents.)

What a Mess!

Hippity Hop's mom says he has to pick up all of his things—NOW!

"All of them?"

Can you find these things for Hippity Hop?

1 train engine

2 soda cans

3 teddy bears

4 balls

5 dinosaurs   **7** train cars   **9** blocks

6 cars   **8** puzzle pieces   **10** crayons

The answers!

page 4 **Lunch Time**
Lunch bag ④

page 5 **Sleepover!**
It's Street ②.

page 6 **Clothesline**

①   ②   ③

page 7 **Here Spot!**

page 9 **Rabbit Reunion!**
25 rabbits

page 10 **Gone Fishing!**
5 fish

page 11 **Lots of Blocks**
9 △ blocks
5 ⌒ blocks
13 ☐ blocks

page 15 **Hippity Hop's Home Video 1**
The missing picture for
① is Ⓑ
③ is Ⓒ and
④ is Ⓐ

page 16 **It's Raining! It's Pouring!**
The raincoat is on the quilt. The rain hat is in the closet. One boot is near the head of the bed. The other boot is near the foot of the bed. The umbrella is on one of the curtains.

page 19 **New Camera**
The close-up pictures are
① sunflower
② bird
③ bunny
④ fish

page 21 **What's Missing?**
① the tail
② the mouth
③ the car door
④ the cake

page 22 **Foursomes**

 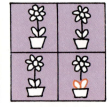

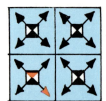 

page 23 **Frog Race!**
Frog ③ wins.

page 26 **Snow Fun**
Twin snowflakes

page 27 **Silly Snowmen!**
Snowman ③ is right.

page 28 **Hippity Hop's Home Video 2**
The missing picture for
② is Ⓑ
④ is Ⓐ and
⑤ is Ⓒ

page 29 **Jelly Bean Machines**
The ① machine that says

Hippity Hop would get 4 beans for his 2 cents.